Zoe's Rescue Zoo

The Silky Seal Pup

Amelia Cobb

Illustrated by **Sophy Williams**

nosy
crow

With special thanks to Natalie Doherty

To Amy x

First published in the UK in 2014 by Nosy Crow Ltd
The Crow's Nest, 10a Lant St
London, SE1 1QR, UK

Nosy Crow and associated logos are trademarks and/or
registered trademarks of Nosy Crow Ltd

Text copyright © Hothouse Fiction, 2014
Illustrations © Sophy Williams, 2014

Printed and bound in the UK by Clays Ltd, St Ives Plc

Papers used by Nosy Crow are made from wood grown in sustainable forests.

ISBN: 978 0 85763 234 0

www.nosycrow.com

That night, Zoe and Meep crept out of the cottage. First they stopped at the seal enclosure to check on Star. The little seal was awake, her eyes shining in the dim light...

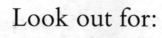

Look out for:

Chapter One

Diving with Dolphins

Zoe Parker splashed through the water, giggling as a playful young dolphin swooped along beside her. It was a warm Friday afternoon at the Rescue Zoo and the last of the visitors had gone home – which meant that Zoe Parker could play with all her animal friends!

As soon as everyone had left the zoo,

Zoe had put her wetsuit on and rushed straight to the lagoon for a swim. There were five bottlenose dolphins at the zoo, who lived together in a small group called a pod. They were some of the cleverest creatures Zoe had ever met – and some of the friendliest too!

As Zoe swam with the pod, the smallest dolphin popped her head above the surface. She chattered cheerfully and Zoe grinned. "I love swimming with you too, Coral," she replied.

Coral gave a happy squeak. Wriggling excitedly, she leaped out of the water, turned a fast, slippery somersault, then dived back in. Zoe laughed as the young dolphin splashed around proudly.

"Hurry up, Zoe. I'm hungry!" squeaked a little voice.

Zoe turned to smile at her best
friend, who was hopping up and down
impatiently at the edge of the water.

Meep was a tiny grey mouse lemur
with huge golden eyes and a long, curling
tail. He was very cute, but also very
mischievous! He went everywhere with
Zoe, except when she went swimming,
because he hated getting wet.

3

"Coming, Meep!" Zoe called to the cheeky lemur. She kicked her way over to the side, with the dolphins splashing along behind her. She climbed out and grabbed a fluffy towel that she'd left on a nearby rock. When she was dry, she pulled her jeans and a jumper over her swimming costume and sat down on the rocks next to Meep. "We'll get you a snack in just a minute," she promised him, stroking his little head. Meep was always ready to eat!

Zoe had lived at the Rescue Zoo ever since she was very small. Her Great-Uncle Horace owned the zoo, and was a famous

animal expert and explorer. While he was
travelling around the world, he'd met lots
of injured, lost and frightened animals,
so he'd decided to turn his home and
gardens into the Rescue Zoo, a home for
any animal in need.

Zoe's mum, Lucy, was the zoo vet,
and Zoe, Lucy and Meep lived in a
cottage on the edge of the zoo, so that
Lucy could help any poorly animal at
any time, even in the middle of the night.
Zoe thought she was the luckiest girl
in the world to live so close to so many
amazing animals.

But there was something even more
special about Zoe. She could *talk*
to animals! All animals can secretly
understand what humans say, but hardly
anyone knows that. Zoe was one of

the few people who could understand animals, and talk to them. But she had to be very careful to keep their secret and only speak to them when there was no one else around.

Coral swam over to the edge of the lagoon and clicked curiously. "I don't know when Great-Uncle Horace is coming back next, Coral," Zoe replied sadly. The Rescue Zoo's owner still travelled around the world looking for animals in danger, and only returned when he'd found a new creature in need of a safe home. "A postcard arrived from Alaska last week – he's been helping a grizzly bear with a sore throat. But it could be weeks until he comes back with the Rescue Zoo's next animal." Reaching down, she stroked Coral's smooth snout and added, "Luckily for me, the zoo already has hundreds of lovely animal friends!"

Meep bounced up and down again. "Zoe, I'm still hungry," the little lemur said hopefully.

Zoe laughed. "All right, Meep, let's go home. I'll come swimming again soon, Coral. Bye, everyone!"

As the dolphins clicked goodbye, Zoe and Meep started wandering back towards the cottage, chatting about all the fun things they could do at the weekend. With all the visitors gone, the zoo was quiet and peaceful. The only sounds Zoe could hear were from the animals around her. The two panda cubs were playing chase in their enclosure. The flamingos squawked, and waved their wings. And

the enormous white rhino, Mwamba,
grunted a friendly greeting as they passed.

Suddenly Meep's ears pricked up.
"Listen, Zoe!" he chattered.

Zoe stopped. Over the snorts, squeaks and whinnies of the animals came a deep growling sound. Zoe had grown up knowing the calls of every single creature at the zoo, and recognised it straight away. It was one of the leopards. But the leopard enclosure was at the other side of the zoo – and this rumbling growl was very close by!

"Do you think Asha or Kafi has escaped, Zoe?" Meep asked nervously.

"We'd better find out. Come on!" Zoe replied, and they rushed down the path towards the sound. Asha and Kafi were her friends, and Zoe knew they'd never hurt her or Meep, but it was still dangerous for a big cat to be loose. And if any of the timid gazelles found out, they'd be *very* frightened.

As they reached the parrot enclosure, there was another giant growl. It sounded as if the leopard was right next to them! Zoe looked around anxiously, but there was no sign of Asha or Kafi's beautiful spotted coats on the pathway or in the bushes around the nearby enclosures.

"I don't understand, Meep," said Zoe, frowning. "Where is the noise coming from?"

Meep scampered to the top of the fence and peered down into the nearest enclosure. "Maybe the parrots will know," he suggested.

Zoe followed Meep up to the enclosure and peered in. It was a large forest enclosure, full of trees. She spotted the scarlet macaw, Ruby, straight away because of her glossy rainbow-coloured

feathers, but it took her a while to spot
Cupid's emerald-green body among
the leaves.

The cheerful lovebird
flapped over to Zoe
and perched on a
branch in front
of her, bobbing
his pink head
up and down
in greeting.
Rio, a white
cockatoo
with a bright-
yellow crest
sticking up
from his head
like a spiky hairstyle,
followed behind him.

Although the birds wouldn't live together in the wild, they liked living together in a friendly flock.

"Have you seen a leopard around here?" Meep called. "We think one might have escaped!"

To Zoe's surprise, the parrots burst out laughing, flapping their bright wings in the air. Then Ruby opened her beak – and made the sound of a leopard growling! Zoe gasped. "It was you!" she said, smiling in relief. "It wasn't a leopard at all. You naughty thing, Ruby!"

The cheeky parrot fluffed her feathers proudly and made a loud trumpeting noise, which made Meep squeal with laughter. It sounded just like Oscar, the African elephant.

Giggling, Zoe waved to the parrots and

carried on down the path, with Meep on her shoulder. As they walked towards the cottage where they lived, the sun began to set, bathing the zoo in beautiful reds and pinks.

Meep yawned sleepily and snuggled against Zoe. "All that swimming has made me tired," he chirped.

Zoe giggled as she cuddled her friend. "You didn't even go swimming, Meep!"

They turned the final corner to the cottage – and suddenly Meep was wide awake again, chattering in glee. Zoe gasped. Outside the cottage, swaying gently in the evening breeze, was a huge, colourful hot-air balloon. Great-Uncle Horace was back!

Chapter Two
The Snowball Seal

Zoe burst into the cottage. "Great-Uncle Horace!" she called as she kicked off her shoes and ran inside. "I can't believe you're back!"

Zoe's mum popped into the hallway. "We're in the living room," she explained in a whisper. "Try to be quiet, love – our new arrival is asleep!"

Zoe's tummy was suddenly full of butterflies. She'd been so eager to see Great-Uncle Horace, she'd almost forgotten that he might have a new animal for the Rescue Zoo! She and Meep grinned at each other. Meeting new creatures was one of their favourite things about living at the zoo.

"What do you think Goo has brought back, Zoe?" whispered Meep excitedly as they tiptoed into the living room. Zoe giggled at Meep's cute nickname for her great-uncle.

Great-Uncle Horace was sitting in a comfy chair with a cup of tea and a plate of his favourite custard cream biscuits next to him. His friendly brown eyes lit up when he saw Zoe. Kiki, the hyacinth macaw who went everywhere with

Great-Uncle Horace, was perched on the back of the chair, preening her beautiful blue feathers. And huddled on Great-Uncle Horace's lap was a ball of pure white fluff.

Meep squeaked curiously. "Zoe, what is it?" he whispered. "It looks just like a big fuzzy snowball."

Zoe grinned. "I think it's a baby seal!"

Great-Uncle Horace beamed. "That's
right, my dear!" he said. "She's a harp seal
pup, and she's just a week old. Come and
have a closer look."

As Zoe and Meep crept forward, the
seal woke up. Slowly, a pair of huge,
inky-black eyes blinked open and stared
at them. Then the baby seal twitched
her black nose and whiskers, and looked
nervously at Great-Uncle Horace.

"She's quite timid," Great-Uncle Horace
explained. "She's had a rather scary time,
I'm afraid. She was taken from her home
by hunters."

Zoe gasped. "That's awful!"

Great-Uncle Horace nodded gravely.
"A baby seal's splendid white coat is very
valuable to some people. Luckily, Kiki
and I found her just in time – and I knew

the Rescue Zoo was the right home
for her!"

Gently, Zoe reached out and stroked
the pup's fluffy white head. "She's so
beautiful," she said.

"And a fascinating animal too!" said
Great-Uncle Horace. "Did you know
that baby harp seals learn to swim and
find their own food when they are just a
few weeks old? Truly incredible. And even
though seals live in some of the coldest
oceans in the world, they're actually
warm-blooded mammals – just like tigers,
or elephants. Their beautiful coats and a
thick layer of blubber keep them toasty
and warm."

Zoe sat cross-legged on the floor in
front of her great-uncle with Meep on her
shoulder. She loved it when Great-Uncle

Horace told her about animals! "What's a group of seals called?" she asked.

"Well, there are a few different names," Great-Uncle Horace replied. "Some people call it a herd, some a rookery, and others a pod."

"Like a group of dolphins!" said Zoe. "That's who we were visiting today, before you arrived." Suddenly a thought popped into her head. "Great-Uncle Horace, why didn't you let anyone know you were coming home? Normally you sail your hot-air balloon right over the whole zoo, so all the animals know you've arrived."

To her surprise, Great-Uncle Horace blushed bright pink. "Well. . .er. . .would you like a custard cream?" he asked quickly, holding out the plate of biscuits.

Zoe glanced down at Meep, who looked just as puzzled as she felt. Was Great-Uncle Horace trying to keep his arrival a secret for some reason? Before she could say anything, her uncle continued. "I almost forgot! I have some more exciting news, Zoe," Great-Uncle Horace smiled. "I've brought home some wonderful chrysalises. They're the little homes that caterpillars make for themselves when they are getting ready to turn into butterflies. They're still in the balloon, and I must take them to the butterfly room at Higgins Hall before they hatch. Would you like to come?"

Zoe hesitated. She loved butterflies, but she was eager to try and speak to the seal pup alone. New animals were sometimes nervous when they arrived at the zoo, and

Zoe always tried to give them a friendly welcome in the special way that only she could! "Can I stay here and help the baby seal settle in?" she asked hopefully.

Great-Uncle Horace nodded, smiling. "Of course, my dear! I know you'll take excellent care of her."

He stood up, with the seal cradled in his arms, and held her out to Zoe. Zoe scrambled up on to the sofa and Great-Uncle Horace carefully placed the seal pup in her arms so she could hold her like a baby. Zoe gasped as she cuddled the little seal.

She was so soft and warm! As Zoe looked
down at her, the pup gazed up with
her big black eyes, her sweet black nose
snuffling curiously. She was absolutely
beautiful!

Before he left, Great-Uncle Horace
turned to Lucy. "I'll see you at the,
er, I mean, *in the morning*," he added
mysteriously.

Lucy walked him and Kiki to the door
and waved them off. Meep hopped on to
Zoe's shoulder. "What's happening in the
morning?" he squeaked.

"I have no idea," Zoe whispered back.
Great-Uncle Horace was acting strangely,
but she wasn't too worried. He was
probably just planning his next adventure.
Anyway, she had other things to think
about – like the gorgeous, silky seal pup!

Chapter Three
The Scared Seal

Once Great-Uncle Horace had left, Lucy popped her head round the living room door. "We'll let the pup sleep here tonight, until Lorna the seal keeper comes to work tomorrow and gets her enclosure ready," she told Zoe. "Can you look after her while I make a bottle of milk?"

Zoe nodded eagerly. As soon as her

mum went into the kitchen, she lowered her voice to a soft, friendly whisper. "My name's Zoe," she told the pup, who was still cuddled up in her arms. "And this is my best friend, Meep."

"I'm a grey mouse lemur," Meep chirped proudly. "What's your name?"

The pup's eyes opened wide. She hesitated, then gave a timid squeak.

"Star? That's such a pretty name," replied Zoe, smiling. "Welcome to the Rescue Zoo, Star."

Star squeaked again, very nervously. Zoe realised the poor little seal was trembling. "No, there are no bad people here," she reassured Star. "The horrible people who snatched you are far away now. Everyone at the Rescue Zoo cares about animals more than anything."

Meep gave a warning squeak as he heard Lucy coming back from the kitchen. Zoe quickly stopped talking.

"Here we go!" announced Lucy, walking in with a bottle. "Do you want to give her the first feed, Zoe?"

"Yes, please!" said Zoe. She loved feeding baby animals! Carefully, she moved Star so she was leaning against one arm, and took the bottle with her free hand. As soon as she offered it to Star, the seal started to gulp hungrily.

"Is this normal milk from our fridge?" Zoe asked.

Lucy shook her head. "It's special milk replacement," she explained. "Seal milk is the creamiest in the world, much creamier than cow's or goat's milk. It's packed full of goodness for seal babies, to help them grow strong and stay nice and warm in the freezing-cold conditions. But because this baby's mum isn't here to provide milk, we'll give her this instead. It's almost as good, although we have to make sure she drinks lots. In fact, we'll need to do night-time feeding, as well as day."

"I'll help," offered Zoe. She wouldn't mind getting up in the middle of the night to feed a gorgeous baby animal like this one!

Star hiccuped as she finished the bottle, and snuggled happily against Zoe's tummy.

"I think she enjoyed that!" said Lucy, smiling. "Now it's time for *our* dinner, Zoe. Pasta for us, and seeds for Meep."

They had dinner sitting on the sofa because Star was still nestled cosily against Zoe and they didn't want to disturb her after her long journey.

"We'll have to think of a name for the seal!" Lucy said as they ate. "Do you have any ideas yet, Zoe? You're always so good at choosing names for our new arrivals."

Meep giggled, and Zoe did her best to hide a smile. She picked the right names because the animals told her what they were called! "How about Star?" she suggested.

"Star the seal. That's very pretty!" said Lucy approvingly.

After dinner, they all cuddled up together to watch a film about blue whales. After a few minutes, Zoe glanced down at Star to make sure the noise wasn't frightening her. But the little pup had fallen fast asleep, her tummy rising and falling gently. Suddenly Zoe found herself yawning.

"Let's watch the rest of the film tomorrow," suggested Lucy. "It looks like everyone needs a good night's sleep! Why don't you and Meep go to bed? I'll set my alarm for midnight so I can give Star her next feed. I promise you can be in charge of her breakfast bottle."

Zoe hugged her mum and gave Star a gentle goodnight cuddle before heading upstairs. She brushed her teeth, put on her green, frog-patterned pyjamas, then climbed into bed. Meep snuggled up next to her, his tiny ears poking out from under the covers. "I like Star!" he chattered.

"Me too," Zoe whispered back. "And I think she likes us, Meep, even though she was so nervous to begin with."

She kissed the top of Meep's soft little head and switched off her bedside lamp. "Goodnight, Meep. We'll have lots of fun showing Star around the zoo tomorrow!"

"*Zoe! Wake up!*"

Zoe blinked sleepily. She'd been having a funny dream about hippos, until a gentle nibbling on her ear had woken her up. Her bedroom was still dark, with moonlight streaming through a gap in the curtains, but Meep was tugging urgently at her pyjama sleeve. "W-what time is it, Meep? What's wrong?" Zoe asked, rubbing her eyes and yawning.

"It's still night-time, Zoe," Meep told her, hopping up and down anxiously. "But I think Star is crying."

Suddenly Zoe was wide awake. She listened, and heard a faint whimpering from downstairs. Meep's clever ears could hear the smallest sounds. "Poor Star!" she whispered, jumping out of bed. "Come on, Meep – but keep quiet, so we don't wake Mum. If we're alone with Star we can ask her what's wrong."

Zoe pulled on her dressing gown and scooped Meep into her arms. She crept

on to the landing and tiptoed down the
stairs, trying not to make them

creak. The cottage
was quiet, but as
she pushed open
the kitchen door
she heard the sad
whimper again.

"Star?" she
asked softly,
flicking on the
light. "It's us, Zoe
and Meep!"

Lucy had made
Star a bed in a box full of cosy blankets,
and the little seal was huddled inside it,
shaking. Zoe rushed over and picked her
up. Star snuggled her soft head against
Zoe's shoulder, sniffling miserably. "What's

wrong? Are you hungry?" Zoe asked, glancing at the clock on the microwave. "It's one o'clock in the morning! Didn't my mum feed you at midnight?"

Star squeaked sadly. Zoe felt her heart melt as the shivering pup explained that Lucy *had* come to feed her, but then she'd left Star all by herself again. And the little seal was scared of the dark!

Meep looked puzzled. His special eyes could see just as well at night as they could in bright daylight! But Zoe understood why the pup was frightened. Sometimes the dark *was* scary, especially if you were in a new place. "It's all right, I promise," she said soothingly. "We're in our lovely, warm cottage. Meep and I are just upstairs, and so is my mum."

Star stopped crying as Zoe cuddled her

close. "That's better," Zoe said, smiling.
"See? There's nothing to worry about.
Let's pop you back in your cosy bed,
and we'll see you in the morning."

The seal pup let out another whimper,
and Zoe saw tears in her beautiful dark
eyes. "Oh, don't cry, Star!" Zoe gasped.

Zoe and Meep glanced at each other.
"What shall we do?" Meep whispered.

Zoe bit her lip worriedly. "We can't
leave her here like this, Meep. But
we can't stay in the kitchen all night
either! We'll have to take her up to my
bedroom."

Star gave a happy squeak and Meep
clapped his tiny hands excitedly. "Shhhh!"
Zoe smiled as she carried them upstairs.

Back in her room, she tucked Star and
Meep up together, and was relieved to

hear a happy sigh from the baby seal.
Then she opened her curtains wide so
that her room was bathed in bright
moonlight. "There. It's hardly dark at all
now!" she whispered to Star. The little
seal's eyes were already starting to close.

Zoe slipped under the covers next to
Star, and the little seal snuggled up to her,
making the most adorable snuffly noises.
As Zoe cuddled her, she wondered what
her mum would say about Star sleeping
in her bed. *I'm sure she won't mind, just
this once*, she thought, crossing her fingers
tightly as she drifted off to sleep.

Chapter Four
The Mysterious Meeting

When Zoe opened her eyes the next morning, something soft, silky and very warm was tickling her neck. The little seal was snuggled up on her pillow, snoring gently. Star didn't seem scared at all with Zoe and Meep to keep her company.

But someone else hadn't slept so well! Meep was curled at the foot of the bed, looking sleepy and cross. "There was no room for me," he grumbled. "I was getting squished!"

Zoe bit her lip to stop herself from laughing. Meep was very funny when he was in a grumpy mood – and even cuter! "I'm sorry, Meep," she soothed. "But we had to help Star, remember?"

Just then the door burst open. Lucy ran in, her face very pale. "Zoe, quick! Star's gone! She must have got out of her box!" she gasped frantically.

Then she spotted the furry bundle in Zoe's bed and gave a sigh of relief. "Oh, Zoe, you gave me such a fright!"

"Sorry, Mum," Zoe said, feeling her cheeks flush pink. "I heard her crying in the night, and she...she didn't seem to like being by herself." Zoe had to think carefully about what to say. She couldn't admit that Star had *told* her she was scared!

"I thought she'd escaped! Really, Zoe, you know she can't sleep with you. You already share your bed with one furry creature," Lucy scolded.

"Yes, and there's no room for another one!" chattered Meep grumpily.

Zoe tried hard not to giggle. "Sorry, Mum," she said again. "But she's going to her enclosure today, isn't she?"

Lucy nodded. "Lorna rang up five minutes ago to say it was ready for her. I thought you could take Star over after breakfast."

Zoe jumped out of bed and gave Lucy a hug. "I will."

Then she noticed Lucy eyeing the bed

warily, and realised what her mum was thinking. "There are no more animals in there, I promise!" she giggled, and Lucy started laughing, too.

Once Zoe had eaten a bowl of porridge and fed Star her bottle, they set off into the Rescue Zoo. Zoe made sure she wore gloves and a woolly scarf, because the seal enclosure was kept at a frosty temperature that was just right for seals but a bit chilly for people!

It was still too early for visitors, so the red-brick paths were quiet. That meant Zoe and Meep could chat to Star as much as they liked. Zoe carried the little seal, and Meep perched on her shoulder. He'd stopped being grumpy now, and was cheerily telling Star about the other animals as they passed them. "That's Sasha," he chattered. "She's a white tiger cub from Siberia. That's a very cold place, like where you come from! And over there are Ernest and Emilie, the anteaters. Aren't their long noses funny?" Meep chuckled to himself as he stuck out his tongue like an anteater.

"And this is your new home!" Zoe added, stopping at a gate in the fence. She reached for her silver paw-print necklace and held it against a panel. With a tiny click, the gate swung open. Zoe was very proud of her special necklace, which had been a present from Great-Uncle Horace. It let her open every gate in the whole zoo, just like the grown-up zookeepers.

Beyond the gate was a huge, deep pool of cold blue water, with chunks of smooth ice floating on the surface, and icy rocks glittering around it. A wide glass tunnel ran along the bottom of the pool so visitors could walk through it to watch the seals swooping and diving right above their heads.

Lorna the seal keeper was inside the enclosure, wearing a wetsuit and holding

a bucket of fish. "She's gorgeous!" she
gasped when she saw the little seal,
reaching out to stroke Star's fluffy head.
"Sally and Finn will be so excited to meet
her."

As she spoke, there was a happy
honking sound from the water. Two sleek
grey heads popped above the surface,
calling a friendly greeting to the new
baby. Sally and Finn were common seals,
with a pattern of dark spots on their
silvery-grey coats.

Star almost jumped right out of Zoe's arms, she was so excited to see them!

Then Sally and Finn dived playfully to the bottom of the pool, and Zoe rushed into the glass tunnel underneath it so that Star could get a better look. Star's dark eyes lit up and she snuffled excitedly as she watched them gliding through the

water, somersaulting with a smooth swish of their flippers and tails. Zoe smiled, relieved the little pup seemed to love her home already.

When they came out of the tunnel, Lorna said, "Let's show Star where she's going to sleep."

There was a row of small, cosy rooms at the back of the enclosure. "This one belongs to Sally," Lorna told Zoe, pointing to the first doorway. "Finn is next door. And this one is for our new arrival."

There was already a snug little bed made for Star. Zoe thought it looked very comfortable, but Star let out a worried wail.

"Oh dear! It sounds like she's ready for a bottle of milk," Lorna said, smiling kindly at the pup. "Come with me, Zoe."

Zoe knew Star wasn't upset because she was hungry. The little seal had realised she had to sleep by herself, and was

feeling frightened about the dark again!
But Zoe couldn't tell Lorna that. Instead,
she followed Lorna into a store room
where all the seals' food was kept. There
were lots of shiny silver fish packed in
crates of ice, and a box of the special milk
replacement for Star. Lorna started filling
up a bottle, humming to herself. While
she was distracted, Zoe tried to make Star
feel better. "There's nothing to be scared
of," she whispered. "Look how lovely your
room is. And you're right next door to
Sally and Finn!"

Suddenly Lorna's walkie-talkie crackled.
"The zoo meeting will start in my office
in five minutes," barked a bossy voice. It
was Mr Pinch, the Rescue Zoo's grumpy
manager. Meep stuck his tiny tongue out
at the walkie-talkie. The little lemur didn't

like Mr Pinch at all! "All zoo staff must be there. Don't be late!" the voice continued crossly.

"What's the zoo meeting about?" Zoe asked Lorna curiously.

Lorna looked flustered. "Oh, nothing to worry about," she said, not quite looking Zoe in the eye. "You know Mr Pinch, always fussing! I'll have to go, but I'll be back soon. Let's leave Star to get to know the others."

Lorna quickly led them out to the poolside and Zoe carefully placed Star on the ground next to the pool. Lorna said a hasty goodbye and left the enclosure. Zoe stared after her. First Great-Uncle Horace was acting oddly, and now Lorna. "What's going on?" she wondered aloud.

"Let's go and find out!" Meep suggested.

Zoe glanced at Star. "We won't be long," she promised the seal, who nodded nervously. "Why don't you explore your home with your new friends while we're gone?"

Sally and Finn had climbed out of the pool and come over to sniff the new arrival. Star wriggled happily towards them. The older seals gave her a friendly nuzzle and then started to show Star around her new home.

Zoe smiled. She didn't feel bad leaving Star when she was having so much fun – but she knew the pup might get frightened again when it got dark. *I'll make sure I'm back before then,* she thought. *But now it's time to find out what this mysterious meeting is about!*

She and Meep ran down the path as quickly as they could, and spotted Lorna taking a shortcut past the zebras. Zoe had to tiptoe after her so that she wasn't seen. She didn't like sneaking about, but she had to know what was going on! As Lorna got to Mr Pinch's office, Zoe and Meep hid behind a tree and watched as all the keepers streamed in.

"Look, Meep! Mum and Great-Uncle Horace are there too," whispered Zoe.

When everyone was inside, Zoe and

Meep crept up to the window and peeped through. Mr Pinch was standing at the front of the room, clearing his throat as if he was about to make a speech. Great-Uncle Horace was next to him, with Kiki perched on his shoulder. Suddenly the old bird spotted Zoe and Meep in the window and squawked in surprise.

Zoe held her breath – if horrid Mr Pinch saw them, she knew he'd tell them to leave immediately. She shook her head urgently at Kiki, hoping she wouldn't make another sound. To her relief, the macaw nodded back.

"Quiet, please!" Mr Pinch announced sternly. "As you all know, the Rescue Zoo has been having some problems with money for a long time. Many of our animals are *very* expensive to look after, and we are not making enough money to keep them all." He glared at the keepers, as if it was all their fault.

A worried murmur went around the room. Zoe frowned, an anxious feeling in her tummy. What did Mr Pinch mean?

Great-Uncle Horace smiled comfortingly. "Now, everyone, there's no need to be alarmed. I came home from Alaska the moment I got Mr Pinch's message, and I'm sure that if we all work together, we'll find a solution." He scratched his head thoughtfully. "Hmm – perhaps we could have a cake sale? I do make a rather splendid carrot cake!"

Mr Pinch frowned. "I am afraid it's *much* more serious than that, Mr Higgins," he snapped. "We have almost no money left. And if we don't find some very soon, the

Rescue Zoo will have to close!"

"What?" gasped Zoe, as Meep gave
a squeak of horror. They stared at each
other in disbelief. The Rescue Zoo
couldn't close!

Chapter Five
The Rescue Zoo
in Danger

The whole meeting fell silent in shock.
The zoo staff seemed as stunned as Zoe
and Meep. "But...but what about the
animals?" asked Will the penguin keeper,
his face very pale.

"They would all be sent to other zoos,"
Mr Pinch announced. "Without the

money to look after them, we would have no choice."

Zoe's heart was thumping fast. *The animals.* All her best friends in the world lived at the Rescue Zoo. There was Bella the polar bear, Oscar the elephant... And of course, there was Meep. Zoe didn't know what she would do without her gorgeous, cheeky little friend, and even the thought of sending him away made her eyes fill with hot tears.

"But we *can't* do that to our animals!" Alison, the bird keeper, exclaimed. "We promised that every creature at the Rescue Zoo would have a safe, loving home here, for ever and ever! We can't make them leave!"

"And what about us?" cried Frankie, the giraffe keeper. "This isn't *our* home, but we love working here. Where will *we* go if the zoo shuts?"

The room was suddenly full of anxious chatter. With a nasty shock, Zoe realised something. The other keepers didn't live at the zoo – but she did! The cottage at the Rescue Zoo was her home. If the zoo closed, there would be no need for a zoo vet any more. Lucy and Zoe would have to leave their beautiful, cosy cottage, and live somewhere else.

Great-Uncle Horace held up his hands for quiet. "Everyone! Please calm down," he said. "The Rescue Zoo *cannot* close. I simply will not allow it. We won't let the animals down. We must all think of a way to raise the money we need. I'm sure we will come up with an excellent plan."

Great-Uncle Horace whipped his green

safari hat from his head. "I'll leave my hat outside Mr Pinch's door. When anyone has an idea, they can write it down on a piece of paper and put it in the hat. At the end of the day, we'll read them all and decide what to do!"

He nodded encouragingly, but the zoo staff looked very upset. Zoe and Meep ducked behind a bench as everyone came out and started trudging back to their animals. Great-Uncle Horace was the last person to leave. He placed his hat by the door, then marched off towards Higgins Hall, with Kiki flying above him. "Time to check on the chrysalises, Kiki old girl!" Zoe heard him say as he rushed away.

"Meep, this is awful!" Zoe burst out. "I can't believe it. Great-Uncle Horace is right – the Rescue Zoo just can't close!"

"I'm scared, Zoe!" the little lemur chirped. His bottom lip was trembling, and his golden eyes were very wide and worried. "I don't want to go to another zoo. I want to stay here with you!"

Zoe gathered him into her arms for a big hug. "And you will, I promise," she told him firmly. "We'll do everything we can to save the Rescue Zoo. We need lots of ideas – and I know who we can ask for help. The animals! Come on, Meep. We'll start with the howlers – they can spread the word!"

The howlers were big, friendly monkeys. Some had bright-red fur, some were pale brown, and some were jet black – but they were all as loud as each other! That was where their funny name came from. Sometimes Zoe could hear them howling when she was shopping with her mum on the other side of town! Zoe and Meep ran to their enclosure and Zoe called over the fence. "We need your help!"

The howlers scampered over quickly. "Can you get a message to all the other animals? Tell them they need to be awake at midnight, for an urgent meeting. I'll explain more then," Zoe told them.

The monkeys looked curious, but nodded. Together they tipped their heads back, took a deep breath and started to give great, gulping howls. Across the path, the warthogs heard the message and started grunting it to all their neighbours, while Ruby and the other parrots started up a noisy chorus. Soon the news about the midnight meeting was being screeched, grunted and roared through the whole zoo!

Chapter Six
The Midnight Meeting

"Time to go, Meep!" whispered Zoe, jumping out of bed.

For the rest of Saturday morning, Zoe and Meep had raced around the zoo, telling all the animals to be ready for the meeting. After that, they'd gone back to the cottage. Zoe had found a notepad and a pencil, and they'd spent the whole afternoon scribbling down ideas. Even when Lucy had sent them to bed, they'd whispered under the covers as the minutes ticked away. Zoe had been sleepy and yawning, but now it was nearly twelve o'clock, she suddenly felt wide awake!

Zoe pulled a jumper over her pyjamas and grabbed her torch. She and Meep listened outside Lucy's bedroom to make sure she was asleep, then sneaked out of the cottage. The zoo was very dark, but Zoe could see a yellow light shining from a window at the top of Higgins Hall. It looked like Great-Uncle Horace was awake. *I wonder if he's thinking of ways to help the zoo, too?* Zoe wondered.

They started walking quickly along the path. "We'll visit Star first," Zoe told Meep. "I want to check she's OK."

Lots of the animals at the Rescue Zoo were nocturnal, which meant they were awake at night, like the bats and the coyotes, who slept in the day and woke up when the stars came out. But tonight every creature was awake for Zoe's meeting, and the path was buzzing with noise. The cheeky orangutans shouted out, wanting to know what was going on. "You'll find out soon!" replied Zoe.

Star was trembling nervously when they opened the door to her enclosure. She gave a happy squeal when she saw them. Zoe couldn't help smiling as she picked the baby seal up and gave her a cuddle. "You can't be frightened of the dark tonight," she told Star, tickling her fluffy tummy. "All the animals are wide awake. Come and see."

The next stop they made was at the parrot enclosure. Zoe unlocked the gate with her paw-print necklace and they slipped inside. Ruby, Cupid and Rio fluttered down from the trees to meet them, and Ruby gave a curious squawk.

Zoe took a deep breath. "The Rescue Zoo is in trouble," she explained to the parrots. "We're running out of money, and if we don't think of a way to make some more, it will have to close down."

Ruby and her friends stared at Zoe, speechless for once. Then they all started squawking anxiously. "Don't worry, we won't let that happen!" Zoe reassured them gently. "But we need everyone to put their thinking caps on if we're going to raise the money we need. Can you fly around and ask the other animals for their ideas?"

Ruby gave a solemn nod. Then she spread her wings and sailed out of the enclosure door into the night air. Cupid and Rio followed, and the parrots flew over the zoo, screeching Zoe's message. As the animals heard the news, there were loud snorts and whinnies of alarm.

Zoe had to call up to the parrots,
"Please, tell everyone to keep quiet! If my
mum or Great-Uncle Horace hear all
the noise, they might come outside to see
what's going on. I'll be in trouble if they
find me out of bed!"

A few minutes later, Cupid fluttered
down on to Zoe's shoulder and squawked
eagerly. "The lions want to have a
roaring contest with the visitors?"
repeated Zoe, hiding a smile. "Hmm...I'm
not sure people would pay to enter that.
But a competition sounds fun."

Rio squawked from the top of the fence,
and Meep squealed with laughter. "The
monkeys think people will pay to have
swinging lessons," the little lemur giggled.

Zoe grinned. "I don't think Mr Pinch
would be very happy if the visitors started

climbing the trees!"

Then Ruby came back from the
hippo enclosure, chattering excitedly.
"Hmmm, visitors won't want to buy the
gloopy mud from their lagoon," said Zoe,
shaking her head. "The hippos might love
wallowing in it, but people would rather
have a nice clean bath. Keep thinking!"

"I know! What about a show?"
Meep suggested, jumping up and down
excitedly. "Lots of people already pay to
see the penguin feeding show!"

"A show is a great idea, Meep!" Zoe
grinned. "But it has to be something
really special and different. Something the
visitors don't normally see."

She paused thoughtfully. Just then, Star
wriggled in her arms and gave a tiny,
adorable sneeze. Zoe giggled and bent

down to rub her cheek against Star's fluffy head. As she did, there was another sneezing sound. It was exactly the same – but this time it hadn't come from Star. Cheeky Ruby had copied it perfectly.

The parrots chuckled to themselves. Zoe laughed too – then stopped as she had a brilliant idea. "That's it, Ruby!" she gasped. "You and your friends could put on a show making the sounds of the other animals! You're so good at it, and it's a really unusual talent. I think the visitors would love it!"

Ruby fluffed her feathers proudly. "And we could sell everyone who comes to the show an information sheet, all about Amazon parrots," Zoe added. "We could put in lots of fun stories about the three of you."

The parrots all squawked approvingly.

Suddenly Zoe's mind started whirring.

"Wait – I have an even better idea," she

exclaimed. "We could sell information

sheets about *all* the animals at the

Rescue Zoo! We can include lots of

Great-Uncle Horace's brilliant animal

facts, and explain where every animal comes from, and what they like to eat."

Meep clapped his tiny hands eagerly. "I want to help, Zoe!" he said, bouncing up and down.

Zoe felt so excited, she wanted to start right away! Suddenly she heard a tiny snoring sound. To her surprise, she saw that Star had fallen asleep, curled up peacefully in her arms.

"I think we'd better take this little one back to her own bed," she whispered to the parrots. "Thank you for everything."

The parrots nodded, looking very pleased and proud to have helped.

Zoe and Meep wished the parrots goodnight and started walking back to the seal enclosure, chatting quietly so they didn't wake Star. Zoe couldn't keep the smile from her face. They had come up with *two* brilliant ideas for saving their home. Now it was time to put them both into action!

"We'll start first thing tomorrow morning, Meep," Zoe whispered eagerly. "There's no time to lose!"

Chapter Seven
Zoe and Meep
Get to Work!

On Sunday, Zoe and Meep ran to
Higgins Hall after breakfast. They
couldn't wait to see what the Rescue
Zoo's owner thought of their ideas!

"Great-Uncle Horace?" called Zoe,
pushing open the enormous oak front
door. "It's me!"

Higgins Hall was hundreds of years old. It had once been a grand house, with huge paintings on every wall, an enormous library and even a maze in the garden. But when Great-Uncle Horace had started the Rescue Zoo, he'd turned every room into a home for different animals. The great white pelicans lived in the swimming pool, and in every bathroom there was a different type of lizard. Great-Uncle Horace had only kept the cosy attic for himself and Kiki.

"Zoe? I'm in the butterfly room, my dear," called a cheerful voice.

The butterfly room had once been a beautiful ballroom. Now it was warm and steamy, with trees and tropical flowers growing in huge pots all around. When Zoe and Meep walked

71

in, Great-Uncle Horace was standing in the middle of the room, with colourful butterflies perched along his arms and on his head. Hundreds more fluttered above him. Zoe felt something tickling her cheek as a pretty purple butterfly came to say hello. She held up her hand and the butterfly settled on her finger.

"It's nice to see you both so early," said Great-Uncle Horace, beaming at them. "But is everything all right, Zoe? You look rather anxious."

Zoe suddenly felt like crying. She'd been brave for all the animals, but now she gave a big sob. "I know the zoo is in trouble," she sniffled. "I listened to the meeting in Mr Pinch's office yesterday."

"Oh, Zoe, you don't need to worry," Great-Uncle Horace sighed, putting his arm round her shoulders and giving her a comforting hug. "I'd hoped you wouldn't find out, my dear, because I didn't want you to get upset. I promise everything will be all right."

Zoe dried her eyes as she looked at Great-Uncle Horace. His kindly eyes twinkled as he gave her a big smile.

"Now, why don't you come and see
my chrysalises..."

Zoe frowned as Great-Uncle Horace
wandered across the room, chattering
excitedly about the chrysalises.

She looked at the three papery packets
hanging from a tree branch, but her mind
was full of the money-making ideas the
animals had come up with. They had
to save the zoo! Turning to Meep, she
whispered, "Let's go and talk to Mum
instead." She said a hurried goodbye to
Great-Uncle Horace and slipped back
outside.

On their way to find Lucy, they stopped
to peer into the seal enclosure. Zoe felt
even more worried when she saw Star's
tired face. While the other seals played
in the water, Star was lying on a rock

sleepily. The little seal explained that
she hadn't felt afraid of the dark when
she was in the parrot enclosure, with so
much friendly chatter around her. But
she'd woken up once she was back in her
enclosure, and had felt frightened again.
She hadn't managed to sleep another
wink all night.

Zoe felt so sorry for her. "I promise I'll
find a way to help you," she told the sad
little seal. "But first I have to help save the
zoo."

Zoe and Meep found Lucy in Oscar's
enclosure. She was halfway up a ladder,
rubbing special cream into one of the
elephant's huge, flapping ears. "Hi, Zoe!"
she called. "Poor Oscar scratched his ear
on a branch this morning, so I'm making
sure it doesn't get sore."

Zoe waited for her mum to climb back down the ladder. "Mum," she said as Lucy reached the bottom, "I know the Rescue Zoo needs money."

"Oh, Zoe, I didn't want you to worry about the zoo closing down. We're going

to do everything we can to save it. We're
going to have a big fundraiser and raise
lots of money."

Zoe felt her heart lift at the thought of
a fundraiser. As soon as people saw how
brilliant the Rescue Zoo was they were
bound to give them lots of money!

"I want to help," she said bravely. "I've
already got some money-making ideas!"

She told Lucy about the parrot show
and the information sheets. "Brilliant!"
Lucy said, smiling. "Why don't you use
my laptop to start writing the sheets?
When I get home tonight, I'll help you
add the Rescue Zoo hot-air-balloon logo
to each one, so they look really smart."

Zoe was so relieved that her mum
thought her ideas might help the Rescue
Zoo. She and Meep rushed back to the

cottage, determined to get started. They sat at the kitchen table and Zoe switched on the laptop.

"Let's start with Oscar," Zoe decided. Great-Uncle Horace had taught her all about African elephants, and she'd learned lots more because she had spent so much time with her biggest animal friend. She opened a fresh page and wrote Oscar's name at the top. "I'll say that elephants are the biggest land mammals in the world. Oscar is seven, but he'll get even bigger until he's about ten. What else can we tell visitors about him?"

"Write about his trunk!" chirped Meep.

"Good idea, Meep," said Zoe, typing quickly. "African elephants have very clever trunks, which can suck up water and pick up food."

"Let's put what he eats," suggested Meep, jumping up and down.

Zoe nodded. "Elephants are herbivores, so that means they eat plants, roots and fruits. Oscar's favourite treats are oranges and bananas."

"And he likes to be tickled behind his ears!" added Meep.

"Perfect, Meep!" said Zoe, writing the last line. "Now, what about the giraffes?"

The two friends worked hard all day, and only stopped for a quick lunch when Zoe heard Meep's tummy rumbling.

When they heard Lucy arriving home, Zoe was finishing a sheet about Star. "Mum, come and read what we've done!" she called.

Lucy sat at the kitchen table and looked through all the sheets, with Zoe perched on her knee. When she got to the very last one, she read it aloud. "*Star the harp seal. Star is the Rescue Zoo's newest animal. She likes milk and being cuddled, but she's still very nervous of people. We're trying hard to show her that the Rescue Zoo is her home now.*" Tears sprang into her eyes and she pulled Zoe into a tight hug. "These are wonderful,

Zoe. I know that when people read them, they'll realise just how special the Rescue Zoo really is!"

Chapter Eight
Parrot Practice

As soon as the school bell went on
Monday afternoon, Zoe rushed back
home to the Rescue Zoo. She and the
parrots had a show to practise for!

Zoe and the keepers had spent all of
Sunday arranging the fundraiser. They'd
put colourful posters all around Zoe's
town to tell people about it, and every

keeper was planning their own special event or stall.

Annie, the parrot keeper, had been happy for Zoe to do a show with Ruby, Rio and Cupid, and had even suggested they have it on the patch of grass near the gift shop, where all the visitors could come and see it. Zoe had been careful not to give away too much about what the clever parrots could do. She wanted it to be a surprise!

Zoe ran into the cottage and dumped her bag on the kitchen table. "Meep!" she called. She listened, but there was no scamper of paws as Meep ran to greet her. *That's strange*, Zoe thought. Meep was *always* waiting for her after school.

Zoe wandered out into the zoo. As she got closer to the parrot enclosure she could hear cross squawking.

Meep was standing on a fence on the outside of the enclosure, talking to Ruby and the others.

"There you are, Meep!" Zoe called in relief. Meep bounded off the fence and into her arms for a cuddle.

"I was helping!" he chattered happily.

Ruby gave an indignant squawk and ruffled her feathers.

Zoe laughed. "Ruby says you were being a very bossy lemur!"

"I wasn't!" Meep protested.

Ruby opened her beak and did a perfect impression of Meep's bossy chattering.

Zoe stifled a giggle. "Never mind, I'm here now," she said. "And we've got a show to plan!"

Zoe unlocked the parrot enclosure with her paw-print necklace, and she and Meep slipped inside. "I think we should have a flying bit, and then your impressions—"

Zoe stopped talking as a group of visitors came up the side of the enclosure. As they peered in she felt like one of the animals! She picked up the parrots' food bowl and pretended to be filling it.

Finally the visitors left and Zoe turned to the parrots. "OK, if we start with Ruby—"

Rio gave a warning squawk and Zoe stopped talking just as the door to the enclosure opened.

"Oh, hello, Zoe," Annie said cheerfully. "I didn't know you were in here. Are you practising for the show?"

"Er, yes," Zoe replied awkwardly.

"You should use hazelnuts," Annie suggested. "Rio will do anything for them." She pulled one out of her pocket and held it up. With a flutter of wings, the cockatoo landed on her arm and picked the nut out of her fingers with his clever feet.

Annie started sweeping the enclosure, and Zoe turned to Meep. "It'll be difficult to have our rehearsals while Annie is here. I can't talk to the parrots in front of her," she whispered to Meep. "We can't start practising while all the visitors are wandering around either..." Zoe looked round the enclosure as she wondered what to do. Then, as she glanced over to the seal enclosure, she thought of Star and had an idea. "Of course! Let's practise at night, once the zoo's empty!"

That night, Zoe and Meep crept out of
the cottage again. First they stopped at
the seal enclosure, to check on Star. The
little seal was awake and whimpering, her
eyes shining in the darkness. Zoe scooped
her up for a cuddle. "We're going back
to see the parrots. You're going to see the
very first rehearsal for their show," she
told her. Star cheered up straight away,
squeaking happily.

Once they'd slipped inside the parrot
enclosure, Zoe explained her ideas for the
show. The parrots listened eagerly, their
heads cocked to one side. "I'll pick an
animal, then you can make the sound,"
Zoe suggested. "Let's start with…a wolf,
like Luna and her cubs!"

Ruby let out a loud, deep howl. It sounded so real, Zoe almost believed one of the wolves was standing next to her! "Warthog," she said. Rio oinked noisily. Meep fell off his log laughing, and Zoe was delighted to see Star giggling shyly.

"When we do the real show, I'll ask the audience to think of some animals too," Zoe explained. "After that, I thought you could do some special tricks! Why don't you start by flying in a pattern?"

Ruby bobbed her head up and down excitedly. Then she squawked to her friends, and the parrots sailed into the air. They flew along in a perfect line, then around in three neat circles. It was going really well until Ruby and Rio tried to land on the same branch and almost crashed into each other!

One by one, they perched on the branch, gripped the bark with their strong claws and swung upside down, which made Star gasp. Finally they flew down and landed in a row on Zoe's arm.

Zoe pulled out a bag of hazelnuts from her pocket and offered the clever birds one each. "That was brilliant!" she told them as they munched the nuts happily.

"With a few more rehearsals it's going to be perfect! I didn't know how talented you were. I can't wait for the visitors see you in action."

As the parrots chatted about more tricks, Zoe grinned. She was sure the visitors were going to love the show. Clever Ruby and her friends might just save the Rescue Zoo!

Chapter Nine
The Big Day

For the next few days everyone at the
Rescue Zoo rushed around getting ready.
The paths were swept, the fences were
painted and lines of cheerful bunting were
hung between the trees. Zoe raced home
from school every day to help and every
night she crept into the zoo, collected Star,
then helped the parrots rehearse.

Mr Pinch had been bossier than ever. He marched around with his clipboard, snapping orders. But he couldn't find a thing to complain about, because as well as the zoo staff working extra hard, the animals were being especially tidy. The keepers noticed it too. "The orangutans swept up all the empty peanut shells in their enclosure today," commented Stephanie, the large-mammal keeper. "It's almost as if they know about the fundraiser, and want the zoo to look its best!"

Zoe and Meep winked at each. Of course, the animals *did* want to do everything they could to save their home!

When Zoe woke up on Saturday, the delicious smell of baking was drifting through the zoo. "Yum!" chirped Meep,

poking his little nose above the covers.
"What's that?"

"I think Great-Uncle Horace has been
making carrot cake!" said Zoe. She
hopped out of bed and looked outside. It
was a sunny morning, and Zoe thought
the Rescue Zoo looked even more
beautiful than usual.

Great-Uncle Horace had set up a table
in front of Higgins Hall, and was piling it
high with tasty-looking cakes and biscuits
to sell to hungry visitors. Outside the
penguin enclosure, Will was organising
a lucky dip. Frankie had stuck up a life-
size drawing of a giraffe, and was going
to colour in his long neck as the day
went on, to show how much money had
been raised. Next to the lake, Annie was
putting out chairs for Zoe's parrot show.

Zoe smiled at how lovely her home looked, but she felt nervous too. Everyone had worked so hard – especially the parrots. They had practised for hours every night, and were keen for every trick to be perfect! Zoe just hoped it was all worth it. After all, today was their only chance to save the Rescue Zoo.

"Come on, Meep," she said, trying her best to sound cheerful. "We've got to put out our information packs before the visitors arrive!"

Zoe got dressed and rushed downstairs. Lucy had just finished printing the packs off, and was stuffing them into a big rucksack for Zoe. She'd added a picture of each animal to the front, and a price sticker in the corner. They looked even better than Zoe had hoped.

Zoe and Meep sped around the zoo, placing the packs outside each enclosure. As they dropped off the very last ones at Star's enclosure, Zoe heard a grumpy voice and her heart sank. "Trust you two to be making a mess on a day like today! Why are you leaving bits of paper all round the zoo?" Mr Pinch snapped.

The grumpy zoo manager snatched up a copy of the pack that Zoe had written about Star and peered at it suspiciously. Zoe held her breath. If Mr Pinch stopped her selling them, all their hard work would have been for nothing! But Mr Pinch looked surprised, then gave a small nod. "I see. This is quite a good idea. Well done, Miss Parker," he said awkwardly. "I'm glad to see you helping out."

As he marched off, Zoe and Meep stared after him in disbelief. Mr Pinch *liked* their idea? "Zoe, I think that was the first time Mr Pinch hasn't told us off!" chirped Meep.

"I know. I can't believe it!" Zoe replied. "Well, if *Mr Pinch* likes the packs, the visitors should too."

Just then Lorna rushed past, speaking into her walkie-talkie. "Those posters seem to have done the trick. There are hundreds of visitors queuing to come inside!" she was saying.

Zoe and Meep grinned at each other hopefully. Lots of visitors was exactly what they wanted today!

Within five minutes of the gates opening, the zoo was bustling and buzzing with noise. People crowded outside each enclosure, chattering excitedly about the animals. There were queues for the raffle and the bouncy castle. Best of all, everyone seemed to love the information packs! Zoe felt really proud when she saw people reading them curiously.

Everything seemed to be going to plan – but Zoe couldn't hang around for very long. It was time to get ready for the parrot show!

At twelve o'clock, Zoe and Meep met Annie outside the parrot enclosure. "I can't wait to see the show!" Annie said as she unlocked the gate. "You've been very mysterious about it."

Ruby, Cupid and Rio were already waiting for them, their beady eyes bright and excited. With an eager chirp, Ruby fluttered on to Zoe's arm, while her friends perched on Annie's shoulders. The crowds on the path gasped as they walked back outside and headed towards the lake. "Aren't they beautiful? And they look so intelligent!" Zoe heard one lady comment.

"They *are* very smart! And they're just about to do a special show. If you'd like to watch, follow me," explained Zoe, smiling at the lady.

Soon all the seats by the lake were filled, and more curious visitors were gathering around. Zoe stood at the front, with Ruby perched on her right arm, Rio on her left and Cupid on her head. As the crowd stared at her, she suddenly felt a bit nervous. Then she spotted her mum and Annie standing together at the back, and they both gave her a huge smile. She took a deep breath.

"Welcome to the Rescue Zoo's first ever parrot show!" she called. "My name is Zoe, and this is Ruby, Rio and Cupid."

As Zoe introduced each parrot, they spread their wings and bobbed their heads, as if they were taking a bow. "Look, Mum! They know their names!" said a little girl in the front row.

"They're very clever birds," Zoe announced. "They all came to us because they were being kept as pets, and they weren't getting the care they needed. In fact, they're just as smart as...an elephant!"

Ruby let out a loud trumpeting noise, and the audience gasped. "That was so real!" said a man in the second row, sounding very impressed.

"And...a lion!" said Zoe.

Cupid gave a powerful roar. It sounded so surprising, coming from his small orange beak! "Goodness me. That's amazing!" a lady in the crowd told her friend.

"And even a whole troop of chimpanzees!" added Zoe.

Together, the parrots screeched and chattered noisily like the zoo's chimps. The audience burst out laughing. Then, with Zoe's encouragement, they started calling out the names of more animals. The parrots hooted, clucked, growled and grunted, with the crowd cheering them on.

Then, with a nod from Zoe, the parrots leaped into the air and started their flying routine. They zoomed right around the crowd, and hung upside down from the trees surrounding the lake. Finally Zoe held out a box of seeds to three children in the crowd and asked them to take a handful each. The parrots hopped up on to the children's heads, leaned down and gently pecked the seeds out of their palms, making them giggle.

Everyone in the crowd stood up and clapped the clever parrots.

"I want to watch them again!" said one excited boy. "I love the parrot show!"

Zoe smiled at the crowd. "I'm glad you've all enjoyed it. If you'd like to see the parrots again, please help us to keep the Rescue Zoo open." She held up a bucket with DONATIONS written on it.

Lots of people put coins into the bucket as they left, chattering excitedly. Lucy and Annie rushed over to Zoe. "That was amazing!" spluttered Annie. "I can't believe how clever our parrots are."

"Well done, Zoe. You were brilliant," added Lucy proudly.

Zoe peered into the bucket hopefully. It felt heavy! Lucy started to count it up and Zoe held her breath. "Well?" she asked as her mum finished counting.

"Well what?" Lucy said confusedly.

"Is it enough to save the zoo?"

"Oh, Zoe." Lucy shook her head and Zoe's heart sank. "You've done *so* well, but the Rescue Zoo needs a lot more money than this. We'll have to see how the rest of the fundraiser goes."

Zoe nodded sadly.

"You did a great job," Lucy said gently, "and everyone enjoyed the show – including the parrots! That's all that matters."

"I think we should make it a weekly event!" Annie suggested brightly. "That is ...if the zoo doesn't close," she added, her face falling a little.

As they packed the parrot show away, Zoe noticed her mum glancing at her watch and looking around anxiously. "What's wrong?" she asked.

Lucy sighed. "I don't know where Great-Uncle Horace is," she explained. "There are lots of reporters here today, and he's meant to be giving a speech outside the lion enclosure in five minutes. If the reporters write about the Rescue

Zoo in their newspapers, people all around the world will know how important it is. They might even send money to help keep it open!"

"Great-Uncle Horace might be selling cakes at his stall," suggested Zoe.

Lucy shook her head. "He disappeared a while ago, and no one's seen him since."

Suddenly Mr Pinch bustled over. "The reporters have started to arrive," he hissed. "Where is Mr Higgins? If he doesn't show up soon, I'll have to make the speech myself!"

Zoe and Meep glanced at each other anxiously. If grumpy old Mr Pinch talked to the reporters, it would be a disaster! Where *was* Great-Uncle Horace?

Chapter Ten
Chrysalis Surprise

As Annie took the parrots home, Zoe
and Lucy followed Mr Pinch to the lion
enclosure. Zoe wanted to ask her animal
friends if they'd seen Great-Uncle Horace,
but there were too many visitors around.
So Meep scampered along the tops of
the fences, calling down to them. "Has
anyone seen Goo?" he chattered. "It's very

important!" But no one had.

Zoe held her breath as Mr Pinch strolled importantly to the front of the crowd of reporters. "Quiet, please!" he said bossily. "My name is Percy Pinch. I am the zoo manager here at the Rescue Zoo. As you can see, I run a very tight ship. Messiness is not allowed! I'm sure your readers will be interested to know what a tidy place the Rescue Zoo is." He nodded smugly.

Zoe heard Lucy groan under her breath. This was awful! Mr Pinch wasn't making the zoo sound like a fun, exciting, special place. She glanced around and saw one of the reporters yawn, and another check his watch. *Great-Uncle Horace, where are you?* she thought desperately.

Mr Pinch took a deep breath, but he was interrupted by a squawk from the

air. Zoe looked
up, her heart
thumping.
It was Kiki!
The beautiful
macaw landed
in a nearby tree, and
suddenly Great-Uncle
Horace came rushing
down the path.

"Thank goodness!" Lucy whispered
to Zoe.

"I'm so sorry, everyone. I'm terribly
late, aren't I? I'll explain why in just
a moment!" Great-Uncle Horace
announced, beaming. "My name is
Horace Higgins, and I am the owner
of the Rescue Zoo. Thank you to Mr
Pinch here for that, er, interesting start."

He tipped his safari hat to Mr Pinch, who looked annoyed at having been interrupted.

Great-Uncle Horace smiled at the reporters. "I hope you have all had a chance to explore the zoo. I am sure you will agree that it is a truly special and wonderful place. I have travelled all around the world, and I can assure you that there is nowhere else quite like the Rescue Zoo! Every creature who needs a home will find one here, from the biggest elephant to the smallest caterpillar." His eyes twinkled. "And speaking of caterpillars, I'd like to show you all something very exciting. Follow me, please!"

He set off in the direction of Higgins Hall. Muttering curiously, the reporters followed, with Zoe, Lucy and Meep at the back. "What's going on?" Zoe asked her mum.

Lucy squeezed Zoe's hand excitedly. "I don't know. But it looks like Great-Uncle Horace has something up his sleeve!"

The crowd piled through the doors of Higgins Hall, and Great-Uncle Horace led them into the warm, colourful butterfly ballroom. Zoe suddenly knew why he'd brought everyone here, and her heart sank. *Oh, no.* He was going to show the reporters the chrysalises! What was so interesting about them?

But Great-Uncle Horace was pointing at three *empty* chrysalises. Fluttering just above them were three very small butterflies, about as big as Zoe's littlest fingernail. Their delicate wings were

a deep rose-pink
colour, with flecks
of pure white in
the middle. "Meet
the Rescue
Zoo's newest
creatures,"
Great-Uncle
Horace announced.
"I discovered their
chrysalises last week, in Alaska. I brought
them back to the zoo and they hatched
just half an hour ago. That's why I was
late for my speech!"

The reporters nodded, but they didn't
seem very excited. Then a short, bald
man pushed to the front of the crowd and
gasped. "I'm from *Buzz Weekly*, a special
insect magazine," he explained. "I've never

seen this type of butterfly before!"

"That's because *no one* has seen this butterfly before. This is a brand-new species!" said Great-Uncle Horace proudly. "I suspected this when I found them, but I couldn't be certain until they hatched. I think they might be the smallest butterflies in the world, although we'll have to wait until the experts can come and measure them." He glanced around, smiling. "Now, where is my great-niece, Zoe? Is she here?"

Zoe's eyes opened wide in surprise. "I'm here," she said, stepping forward.

"Ah, wonderful. Come here, my dear! There's something else I must tell you about this butterfly." Great-Uncle Horace beamed at Zoe. "Did you know that whenever a new species is discovered, the person who found it is allowed to pick its name?"

Zoe shook her head, feeling puzzled.

"Well," continued Great-Uncle Horace, smiling as one of the new butterflies landed on his finger, "that means I have the pleasure of naming this new species. And I've decided to name it after *you*, my dear. This butterfly will be called *Papilio Zoeana* – 'Zoe's butterfly'."

The crowd started chattering excitedly. Suddenly the room was lit up with everyone taking photos of the butterflies. "This is amazing!" the man from *Buzz Weekly* was saying. "I'm going to write a special feature all about this. Our readers will love it!"

The reporters all started scribbling in their notebooks and making excited phone calls about the news. "Yes, that's right, it may be the smallest butterfly in the world!" one shouted down the phone.

Great-Uncle Horace glanced at Zoe, then bent down, looking concerned. "Zoe, what's wrong? I thought you'd be delighted to have the butterfly named after you."

"I am! But...but I still feel sad," Zoe

explained. "Everyone liked the fundraiser, and my parrot show went well, and the news about the butterfly is really exciting – but we still haven't managed to save the Rescue Zoo. The butterflies won't have a home if we have to close down!"

Great-Uncle Horace shook his head gently. "My dear, I tried to tell you, the Rescue Zoo won't *have* to close down. You see, people will travel from all around the world to see this rare new butterfly. Butterfly experts will come in their thousands. The Rescue Zoo will be famous. Zoe's butterfly has saved the Rescue Zoo!"

As the sun started to set that evening, Zoe and Meep wandered happily through the zoo, sharing a slice of carrot cake.

The last visitors were leaving, chatting about everything they'd seen at the zoo, and promising to come back soon. Will was packing away the lucky dip, whistling cheerily. Frankie was colouring in the last bit of her giraffe picture, to show that they'd reached their fundraising target. Everyone agreed that the day had been a huge success. The zoo was safe – with a little help from Zoe's butterfly!

When the news about the rare arrival had spread through the zoo, the keepers had started cheering and hugging each other. Even Mr Pinch had looked pleased. "Nice, quiet, tidy creatures," he'd commented, nodding. "Yes, I do like butterflies."

One by one, the news had reached the other animals too. The hippos celebrated

by blowing huge bubbles in the mud. The
flamingos squawked happily, and all the
big cats joined together in one giant roar
of delight. Meep was so excited, he hadn't
stopped bouncing around all afternoon!
"Now I can stay here with you!" he'd
chattered gleefully, jumping on to Zoe's
shoulder to give her a big hug. "Hooray!"

The first stars started twinkling above them, and Zoe found herself yawning. "I'm sleepy, Meep! It's been a long day," she told her little friend. "Maybe we should go home. Great-Uncle Horace said the man from *Buzz Weekly* is coming back tomorrow, to write his special piece about the butterfly. He wants to ask me some questions about living at the Rescue Zoo! So we'd better get a good night's sleep."

They started walking back to the cottage, then Zoe stopped suddenly. "Meep," she gasped. "I've just remembered Star! We've been so busy, we still haven't found a way to stop her being scared of the dark!"

"Let's go and see her now!" chirped Meep.

Zoe's tummy turned over as they rushed to the seal enclosure, and she opened the gate with her paw-print necklace. She couldn't believe she'd forgotten about the frightened seal pup! But as they burst into her room, Star lifted her head sleepily.

Zoe thought Star would be trembling, like the last time they'd seen her. But, to her surprise, the fluffy pup seemed perfectly happy!

Zoe bent down to give her a gentle stroke. "You don't look nervous at all!" she said.

The tiny seal nodded proudly. With a contented squeak, she explained that she wasn't frightened any more. She'd spent so many nights watching Zoe and the parrots rehearse for their show, she knew that there was nothing to be scared of at night-time. The Rescue Zoo was a friendly, safe place to live, even in the dark!

Zoe bent down and kissed Star's soft head. "That's wonderful!" she said. "And the Rescue Zoo will be your home for ever. Sleep tight, and we'll see you tomorrow."

Star gave a happy squeak before snuggling back down and closing her eyes. By the time Zoe closed the enclosure gate, the silky seal pup was fast asleep and snoozing peacefully.

Meep jumped into Zoe's arms for a cuddle as they walked back home, and Zoe gave a contented sigh. Every creature at the Rescue Zoo would sleep happily tonight. And now that their home was safe, there would be lots more exciting animal adventures to come!

Look out for more amazing animal adventures at the Rescue Zoo!

The Rescue Princesses

Have you read?

Look out for:

nosy crow